Andi Lassos Trouble

Circle C Stepping Stones

Circle C Stepping Stones #3

Andi Lassos Trouble

Susan K. Marlow

Kregel
Publications

Andi Lassos Trouble
© 2017 by Susan K. Marlow

Illustrations © 2017 by Leslie Gammelgaard

Published by Kregel Publications, a division of Kregel, Inc., 2450 Oak Industrial Dr. NE, Grand Rapids, MI 49505.

ISBN 978-0-8254-4432-6

Printed in the United States of America
17 18 19 20 21 22 23 24 25 26 / 5 4 3 2 1

Contents

New Words

ain't—a poor way of saying "am not," "are not," or "is not"

arena—an enclosed area where sports or other events take place

barbecue—an outdoor picnic where food is cooked over an open fire or on a grill

bronc—a wild, unbroken horse; short for bronco

bunkhouse—a ranch building where the hired hands sleep

chaps—the leather protection worn over a cowboy's trousers

dally—to wind the lasso around the saddle horn after roping an animal

honda—a special loop knot tied at one end of a lasso that allows the rope to slide freely

lariat—another word for a lasso

rodeo—an event where people compete at riding horses and bulls, catching animals with ropes, and other ranch-related skills

shenanigans—foolish, high-spirited behavior; mischief

skittish—jumpy or uneasy; excitable

stampede—when a group of animals rush wildly in a sudden panic

steer—a male animal in the cattle family that cannot father a calf

vaquero—(bah-CARE-oh) the Spanish word for a cowboy

vermin—small animals that are harmful or annoying; pests

⊰ CHAPTER 1 ⊱

In a Pickle

Late Summer 1877

"**H**ey, Sadie, can you do this?"

Andi Carter hung upside down from the lowest branch of an oak tree. Her arms and two dark braids dangled above her best fishing spot.

Well, Andi corrected herself. *It was my best fishing spot four months ago.*

Now the pool held less than two feet of greenish water. The arm-length trout were gone. A few yards away, the creek gurgled slowly downstream.

California summers were not kind to creeks and fishing spots.

Andi spread her arms wide. "I'm hanging here just like the trapeze artists did under the big top."

The excitement of seeing the circus had not faded from Andi's memory even after two weeks. It was too bad Sadie lived up in the hills so far away from town. She had not learned about the circus until after it had come and gone.

Sadie glanced up. "I reckon I could do that if I wanted to." She wrinkled her nose. "But I don't want to." She went back to poking a turtle that lay half buried in the mud. "One slip and you'll end up in that disgusting water."

Andi twisted her neck for a better view of the pool. Just below the surface, tiny minnows darted back and forth. Water bugs skated across the green scum.

The last time Andi pretended to be a trapeze artist, she'd landed flat on her back and got the wind knocked out of her. This time she might end up in a muddy fishing hole.

Sadie's right. This is not one of my best ideas.

Andi reached up and grasped the thick limb with one hand. It was easy to bring her other hand up. However, it was *not* easy to scoot along the branch while hanging upside down. It was harder still to hike herself up so she could sit back up in the tree.

More like impossible, Andi thought, grunting at the effort.

Sadie stood up. "What are you doing?"

"Trying to get out of this tree." Andi scooted a few inches.

"I told you to get that ol' circus outta your head," Sadie said. "But no. It's all you want to play." She shook her head. "You're gonna have to slip your legs off the branch and drop."

"*Drop?* Are you crazy?" Andi's voice rose in horror. "I'll land in that stinky water."

"Better to land in it with your feet than with your head." Sadie came close to the pool's edge. She stuck out her free hand and wiggled her fingers. "I can't reach you. Sorry."

Sadie didn't sound sorry. She sounded glad that Andi was out of reach and couldn't be helped. Glad that her own feet were safe on dry land and not dangling over a mucky water hole.

Andi dragged herself another inch along the branch. Her hands felt sweaty. Her head pounded in time with her heartbeat. *Thump-thump. Thump-thump.*

How had a champion tree climber gotten herself into such a pickle?

You were showing off, a little voice whispered inside Andi's head. *And look where it got you. Stuck upside down in a tree.*

Andi cringed. The words were exactly what her big brother Chad would say if he saw her like this. He would push back his wide-brimmed hat and laugh and laugh.

At least Chad would help me out of the tree after he was done laughing, Andi thought.

11

Her fingers slipped. She gasped and scrambled to keep hold of the branch.

"You can't hang there forever," Sadie said. "Better drop before you fall."

Sadie was right . . . again.

Andi wrinkled her nose. "Oh, all right."

She held on tight and slipped one leg from around the limb. Then she unwrapped her other leg. Hanging on with both hands, she carefully lowered her feet. Water shimmered just below her bare toes. She could almost touch it. *Yuck.*

Andi glanced at the creek bank a few feet away. *Hmm . . .*

She kicked out her legs. "Maybe I can swing back and forth, let go, and jump to the ground."

Sadie looked from Andi to the edge of the pool. "Don't hurt to try, I reckon."

"One . . ." Andi huffed. "Two . . ." Her legs flew toward dry land. *I can do this!*

Her sweaty fingers slipped.

Splat!

Andi landed on her bottom just inches from the pool's edge. Scummy water splashed her face and rose up past her belly. Mud squished between her fingers. "Help!" she shrieked.

Sadie was too busy laughing to help Andi. "Oh, oh, oh!" She doubled over and howled. "You should see yourself."

Andi stood up. Dripping wet, she climbed out of the fishing hole. Green scum stuck to her overalls, to her braids, and to her bare arms. "It's not funny!"

"You're right, it's not," Sadie said. "It's *hilarious!*" She clapped a hand over her mouth to quiet her giggles, but her blue eyes sparkled.

Hot anger boiled up inside Andi. She jammed her muddy fists on her hips and glared at Sadie. Her thoughts spun. *Maybe I don't want to be friends with her anymore.*

Maybe Chad was right. He didn't like Andi going around with a sheepherder girl from the no-account Hollister clan. No, sirree! Just the word "sheep" upset Chad and every other cattle rancher in the valley.

Cattlemen did *not* like sheep. Or sheepherders.

I'm probably better off without a mean, laughing—

"I didn't mean to make you mad." Sadie's apology cut into Andi's thoughts. "It just burst outta me when I saw you in that stinky water. Let me help you wash it off."

Andi's anger cooled. She peeked down at her overalls. They were a muddy, scummy mess. Sadie had good reason to laugh. *I guess it serves me right for showing off.*

She bit her lip. Andi didn't really want to lose Sadie's friendship.

Sadie was lots of fun. She was also the only girl

Andi's age within ten miles of the ranch. "All right. I know a spot upstream where the creek is a little deeper. And cleaner."

Sadie grabbed Andi's hand and gave it a tug. "Come on then."

"Wait a minute." Andi glanced over her shoulder. "We better check our horses first. It's a long way home if Taffy wanders off."

"Don't worry." Sadie swung around and pointed. "They're right where we left 'em."

Andi relaxed. Sadie's horse, Jep, and Taffy stood side by side on the other side of the oak tree. The palomino's cream-colored tail swished flies from Jep's face. Jep's dark-brown tail returned the favor to Taffy.

Satisfied that her horse was staying put, Andi waded into the creek and started upstream.

It didn't take long to find the deeper part of the creek. It ran swift and clean. Andi sat down and let the water ripple over her muddy arms and legs. Then she ducked her head and rinsed her hair.

Drops sputtered from Andi's mouth when she came up for air. She shook the water from her braids and scrubbed her arms clean.

Sadie washed the mud and scum from Andi's back. Then she cupped her hands and threw water in Andi's face.

"Hey!" Laughing, Andi splashed her back.

Ten minutes later, a low, distant rumble paused the water fight.

"Is that thunder?" Sadie asked.

Andi looked up. Not one cloud dotted the sapphire-blue sky. "I don't know." The rumbling grew louder. She wrinkled her forehead. What was that noise?

"It's coming from over there." Sadie pointed toward the distant mountains.

Andi stood stock-still in the middle of the creek. Water dripped down her face. She swiped the drops away and turned to see where Sadie was pointing.

Just then a dark, rolling mass appeared between two hills. The ground trembled.

Andi shaded her eyes. The mass had spread out into heads and horns and legs.

She gasped. "It's cattle, Sadie. And they're coming this way!"

⊰ CHAPTER 2 ⊱

Cattle, Cattle Everywhere

Sadie squealed in terror. "What'll we do?"

Andi couldn't talk. A big lump was stuck in her throat. She stared at the fast-approaching cattle. Then she glanced back down the creek.

Her heart skipped a beat. The horses!

Taffy and Jep stood with their heads up and their ears pricked forward. Jep shook his mane and moved off. Taffy's head bobbed up and down. She looked ready to gallop away.

No!

Andi swallowed the lump and yelled, "Run, Sadie!"

Andi sprang from the creek with Sadie at her heels. Small rocks cut into Andi's bare feet. She cried out but didn't stop. Sadie tripped and fell. Andi pulled her up and they kept running.

The thundering hooves drew closer.

Andi ran faster.

For the first time since she and Taffy had become horse and rider, Andi wished she had tied up her filly. If she could only mount her in time, Taffy would easily outrun the stampeding cattle.

The palomino pranced to and fro. She pawed the ground and whinnied. *Hurry, hurry!* she seemed to be saying.

Sadie scrambled up the oak tree, but Andi headed straight for Taffy. "Don't run away!" she shouted.

Just then, Jep kicked out his hind legs and galloped off.

Andi caught Taffy's reins. "Easy, girl. Hold still." She reached for a stirrup.

Taffy didn't obey. She snorted and sidestepped. Then she jerked the reins from Andi's hand and took off after Jep.

"Up here!" Sadie shouted. *"Hurry!"*

The fear in Sadie's voice sent Andi up the tree without looking back. She passed the branch Sadie sat on and climbed higher. Her breath came in short gasps. She scurried up two more limbs then leaned back against the thick trunk and tried to catch her breath.

"You climb like a monkey," Sadie called from

where she sat straddling a branch. "You didn't have to go so high."

"I couldn't stop." Andi glanced down.

All sizes of cattle stomped the ground under the oak tree. They stood exactly where Andi had been one minute before.

Thank you, God, for trees, she silently prayed.

The cattle snorted and prodded each other for a place at the water. A tan mama cow with a half-grown calf shoved her way between two steers. Another steer stepped in Andi's fishing hole and plunged his nose into the stale water.

Andi pushed the leaves aside and looked out over the rangeland. Where had Taffy gone?

The rushing cattle looked mean enough to scare anybody. They had scared Andi and Sadie up a tree. Maybe they had scared Taffy all the way back to the barn.

Andi scowled. *They better not have!*

Cattle stood drinking along both sides of the creek for as far as Andi could see. Their heavy hooves sank into the streambed. They churned the slow-moving water into a muddy mess.

But at least they had settled down.

Whatever had made the cattle stampede was over. They drank the dirty water then started grazing on the summer-dry grass.

Except for a few calves calling for their mamas,

and one or two cowboys shouting in the distance, it was quiet.

"Those big, fat, dirty ol' cattle," Sadie burst out. "They're trampling your special spot."

Andi clenched her fists and nodded. She was too upset to answer. Chad had given Andi this place for her very own special spot. He said nobody ever came up here.

Not cattle. Not horses. Not ranch hands.

Until today.

Sadie waved Andi down beside her. "Look at 'em," she said when Andi had settled herself on the lowest limb. "Filthy beasts. Whose are they?"

"Ours," Andi said right away. "Whose else would they be?"

"I don't think so." Sadie pointed to the tan cow grazing a few yards away. "That don't look like your brand."

Every cow and bull and steer and horse on the Circle C ranch wore a special mark burned into their rumps. It was a circle with the letter C inside. It made it easy to tell which livestock belonged to the Carter family.

The mark on the tan cow showed LLL.

"That's a Triple L brand," Andi said. She peered closer. "Look, Sadie. Her calf's wearing a different brand—the Bent Pine mark."

Andi wrinkled her forehead and thought hard.

"That doesn't make any sense. They should both have the same brand."

"Nothin' 'bout us being stuck up in a tree right now makes sense." Sadie shook her head. "Worse, our horses took off. How are you and me gonna get home?"

Good question. Andi had no answer.

Just then a cowhand rode up next to the tan-colored cow. He pointed to the calf. "How did that brand get there?"

His angry shout made Andi jump. She didn't recognize him, and she knew every cowhand on the Circle C ranch.

Four other men galloped up. The cattle scattered. Andi scrunched closer to the tree trunk to keep out of sight.

Sadie scooted next to Andi. "Are they cattle rustlers?" Her eyes were wide and scared.

A hard lump dropped into Andi's belly. *Cattle rustlers.* What a terrible thought! She didn't want to be anywhere near outlaws who stole other people's livestock.

Please, God, she prayed, *don't let them be cattle rustlers.*

"I said *how did that brand get there?*" the furious cowhand shouted again.

"How do you think a brand got on a calf, Mack?" A scruffy-looking cowboy riding a spotted horse laughed. "Rope 'em, brand 'em, and they're yours."

Mack shook his head. "Mr. Flanders ain't gonna like seeing a Bent Pine brand on one of his calves, Tate. Not if its mama's wearing a Triple L mark."

"Too bad," Tate shot back. "Mr. Jenkins is paying a bonus for every unbranded calf we bring back to the ranch with a fresh Bent Pine brand." He laughed louder. "I'm just better at steer roping than you'll ever be."

"That'll be the day!" Mack yelled.

Andi let out a breath. God had sure answered her prayer fast. "They aren't cattle rustlers," she told Sadie. "They work for the two ranches near the Circle C."

Sadie huffed. "Then what are they doin' on *your* ranch? They're makin' a mess of your special spot. And their cattle spooked our horses."

Andi didn't know the answer to Sadie's question. The Triple L and Bent Pine cowhands were a long way from their two ranches. And why were their cattle all mixed up together?

Cowboy Tate on his spotted horse looped his rope. Then he swung it over his head. "Now I'll thank you to let me and this-here calf be on our way." With a quick toss, he lassoed the calf.

"That's a Triple L calf and you know it," Mack said.

Tate tightened the loop around the animal's neck. "Don't know nothin' about it. This ain't no day-old nursing calf. It's nearly grown, so it's fair game. I'm gonna—"

Mack flew out of his saddle and tackled the Bent Pine cowboy. Both men crashed to the ground. They rolled over and over. Their hats came off. Fists flew.

Six other cowhands dismounted and formed a ring around the two men. They *yee-hawed* and laughed. Money exchanged hands.

"They're betting on who'll beat up who," Sadie whispered.

Andi watched with wide eyes. Grown men acting like little boys in the schoolyard! Then her mouth dropped open. Two Circle C hands stood with the others, watching the fight.

If big brother Chad saw his men wasting time like this, he'd blow his top.

"That's enough!"

Chad's sudden roar cut through the cowboys' laughter and shouting. He and Sid, the Circle C foreman, pushed through the human ring.

"What in blue blazes is going on here?" Chad hollered.

Up in the tree, Andi bit her lip.

Yep, Chad just blew his top.

⪡ CHAPTER 3 ⪢

Mother's Great Idea

The circle of laughing men grew quiet at Chad's angry words. Sid broke up the fight. Tate and Mack found their hats and limped away.

"You won't tell the boss about this, will you, Mr. Carter?" Tate pleaded. "I need this job."

Mack brushed the dust from his chaps. "It was just a friendly scuffle over a calf."

"Friendly *nothin',*" Chad growled. "This is the third fight this week. What's going on?"

The cowboys all started talking at once.

"The cattle are mixed up worse than ever this year," one yelled. "They're scattered all over the hills. We're workin' ourselves to death trying to sort 'em all out."

"I was just rounding up what's rightly Triple L beef," Mack shouted.

Tate lunged for Mack. "Check the brand. That ain't a Triple L—"

Sid yanked him back. "Cool your heels, boy."

On and on the cowboys grumbled. It was hot, and the cattle were thirsty. Nobody meant to let Triple L and Bent Pine beef get this far onto the Circle C, but sometimes it couldn't be helped.

"They smelled water and rushed the creek before we could turn them, *señor*," Diego said.

Chad eyed the Circle C cowhand. "Our cattle are mixed up in this mess too?" He waved his arm toward the grazing livestock.

Diego nodded. "*Sí, señor*. Some of them."

Chad shook his head. "Wonderful," he muttered.

"No harm done, boss," Wyatt, another Circle C hand, said. "We'll round up our beef and—"

"No harm done?" Chad stepped under the oak tree and pointed up. "You almost got two little girls trampled."

Andi gasped. How did Chad know she and Sadie were up in the tree?

Dumb question. Chad always kept an eye out for Andi. He knew this was her special, private spot.

She frowned. *Not very private today.*

"Come on down, girls," Chad called. "It's safe now."

While Andi and Sadie climbed out of the tree, Chad yelled at the cowhands some more. "You spooked their horses. I saw Taffy. She's halfway home by now. The other horse was right beside her."

"We're sure sorry, Miss Andi," Wyatt said. "We didn't know."

The others nodded. They looked ashamed of themselves.

Chad pointed to Tate and Mack. "You two go after the Hollister girl's horse. Be quick about it, or your bosses will hear about this afternoon's brawl."

When they hesitated, Chad exploded. "Get going!"

The two cowboys jumped on their horses and took off.

"Now, get this beef back where it belongs," Chad ordered the rest of the men.

The group broke up and hurried to obey.

Chad put Sid in charge and then whistled for his horse. Sky trotted over.

"Sid will make sure you get your horse back," Chad told Sadie. He mounted Sky and pulled Andi up behind him.

Sadie nodded, white-faced.

"Sid's nice," Andi said.

Sadie didn't answer. She looked too scared to speak.

Andi knew Sadie was afraid of Sid and the other

27

cowhands. Most sheepherders were afraid of cattle-men. They never knew when someone might try to chase them and their sheep out of the area.

"I'll take Andi home and meet you at the south section in an hour," Chad told Sid. "This day's not over yet." He dug his heels into Sky's sides. The horse leaped into a gallop.

Andi wrapped her arms around her brother's waist and hung on tight. She loved riding with Chad. He always galloped Sky extra fast.

"Good-bye, Sadie!" Andi yelled over her shoulder.

Sadie waved. She looked tiny and lonely standing by herself under the tree.

⤝ ⤞

"Well, that's the long and short of it," Chad said at supper that night. He leaned back in his chair, crossed his arms, and let out a big breath. "It feels like this roundup's taking forever."

"It sure does," Mitch agreed. He looked as tired and worn out as Chad. "Whenever our men mix with the Triple L or Bent Pine hands, fights break out."

"What are they fighting about?" Mother asked.

Chad shrugged. "Oh, the usual. Who can rope and ride the best. Who's faster at cutting a steer from the herd. Or who can tie up and brand a calf the quickest."

"I see," Mother said thoughtfully. "It appears the men are trying to outdo each other to prove which of them is the top cowhand."

"Yep." Mitch nodded. "Just like they do during every roundup. Only this year it's gotten out of hand."

"Like today." Chad frowned. "They let part of the herd get away from them and"—he looked at Andi—"it could have ended badly."

Andi perked up at being included in the table talk. "Those cows trampled all over my special spot," she said, scowling. "They muddied the water and scared Taffy."

"I heard they scared you and Sadie right up a tree," Melinda said. She dabbed her mouth with a napkin. "If you stayed indoors instead of galloping around the countryside like a wild—"

Mother cleared her throat, and Melinda fell silent.

Andi kept quiet too, even though she wanted to tell her big sister a thing or two.

Ever since Melinda had learned she would be attending a young ladies' academy in San Francisco this fall, she'd acted more prim and proper than ever. Melinda was too busy to go riding. Too excited about the new school year to listen to Andi's chatter. Too eager to scold Andi when she—

Andi sighed. *I thought I'd miss Melinda, but*

maybe I won't. Not if she keeps putting on "fine lady" airs day and night.

"Perhaps the men need something to look forward to," Mother went on as if Melinda had not spoken.

"Something more than their pay?" Andi's oldest brother, Justin, raised his eyebrows. "They earn top dollar. And the Triple L and Bent Pine ranches pay the same as we do."

Chad stopped chewing. He took a swallow of water and pointed his fork at Justin. "You've forgotten what hard work is like."

"He sure has." Mitch grinned. "Maybe big brother should leave his soft lawyer chair and do a *real* day's work for a change."

Laughter rippled around the table.

Justin didn't join in. "I've done my share of—"

"You might add a spark of fun to these roundup tasks," Mother interrupted cheerfully. "Perhaps the Circle C could host a rodeo contest to celebrate the end of the season."

A rodeo? Andi thought.

"A rodeo?" Chad said out loud. He rubbed his chin and nodded. "Yes, that might work. We've got a week or two left of roundup. The hands could work on perfecting their skills."

"It might cut down on the quarrels," Mitch agreed. "Especially if the men knew they could show off their roping and riding in an arena." He smiled. "Good idea, Mother."

Andi thought it was a *great* idea. She thought it was an even better idea when she heard the rest of the plans. Chad would invite the Triple L and Bent Pine ranches to help organize and compete in the contest.

Three ranches trying to prove their cowboys were the strongest and best in the valley. There would be prize money and trophies. And a big barbecue for anybody in the valley who wanted to come and watch.

Mitch smacked his lips. "We'll roast a couple of steers over that big pit out back."

Andi's mouth watered at Mitch's suggestion. Then another idea sent prickles racing up and down her arms. Maybe she and Taffy could enter a contest.

Andi smiled to herself. She was *very* good with a lasso.

Yes, a rodeo sounded like the most fun in all of California!

⊰ CHAPTER 4 ⊱

Bunkhouse
Chatter

Andi skipped out of the barn with a coil of rope looped around her shoulder.

Right next door a dozen cowhands relaxed on the bunkhouse porch. The last rays of the setting sun shone across their excited faces. They joked and laughed and boasted about their roundup skills.

Andi hurried over. *News sure travels fast on a ranch!*

Supper had ended only an hour ago, and already the men were buzzing about the rodeo. By tomorrow night the Triple L and Bent Pine cowboys would be talking about it too. By next week most of the valley would know about the Circle C's upcoming barbecue and cowboy contest.

Andi squeezed past the sprawling cowhands and sat down on the porch. She wrapped her arms around her drawn-up knees and listened to their excited chatter.

"*O sí,*" Diego was saying. "I was a young *vaquero* in those days. I have not seen such grand rodeos since then. My older brother"—he sighed—"such a bull rider he was. A champion."

Andi caught her breath in horror. Who would be crazy enough to ride a bull?

Chad had pointed out Montaña to Andi once or twice. The Circle C's mountain of a bull was kept far away from the house and yard. Montaña looked mighty mean, even for a prize bull.

I wouldn't sit on his back for anything!

"Who can beat out those other ranches at calf roping?" Wyatt asked.

Andi put the scary thought of riding a bull out of her head. Roping a calf sounded much easier. Safer. And something she could do.

The cowboys broke into loud discussion. Three or four held up their hands. "Roy's the fastest," one said.

"I can rope a calf," Andi said, holding up her lasso. "If it's small enough."

Wyatt chuckled. "We know you can, Miss Andi, but you don't just toss a rope 'round its neck. You gotta tie it down too."

"Like you're gonna brand it," Clay put in.

Andi ducked her head. "Oh." *No calf-tying contest for me.* She sighed and dropped her lasso on the porch's wooden floor.

Diego bent close to Andi's ear. "Do not look so glum, little one. Perhaps *Señor* Chad will include a contest to rope a calf, *no?*"

"Sure," Clay said. "I bet there's plenty of young'uns who'd want to join the fun. Horse racing and calf roping sound just right for your size."

Andi perked up. "I could race. Taffy's the fastest filly ever. And I don't weigh much."

Two cowboys laughed and ruffled Andi's hair. Then they went back to talking about the other contests.

Who could win the bronc-riding contest? Would Mr. Jenkins bring Firebrand, the Bent Pine's unbreakable, crazy-wild stallion? His coat was as red as his temper.

"Jenkins boasts that *nobody* can stay on Firebrand," Clay said.

Wyatt snorted. "Ain't a horse that can't be rode—"

"Never a cowboy that can't be thrown," Clay shot back. "Do you reckon Chad will give Firebrand a try?"

"Oh, yeah!" Wyatt said.

Andi shivered. Riding a bucking bronco sounded scarier than riding a bull.

"What about the team roping?" young, curly-haired Roy asked. "Takes two to catch and tie down a full-grown steer."

Diego whistled softly. "I have never seen any two do it better than the *señores* Chad and Mitch."

There were nods all around.

On and on the cowhands talked. The sun dipped lower, but none of the men looked ready to break up the gathering and head for bed.

Andi's smile stretched from ear to ear. From team roping to calf roping to bull and bronc riding, the Circle C cowboys had already won the rodeo with their words. How much harder could it be to win it for real?

Not hard at all from the way Diego boasted of long-ago rodeo victories. "I am far too old to compete in this contest," he said. "But I can give you good advice if you are willing to listen."

"Tell me how to win at calf roping, Diego," Andi burst out.

The Mexican *vaquero* smiled. "You must choose a horse who knows what to do as soon as the rope tightens around the calf's neck," he said. "And practice, practice, practice throwing your lariat."

Andi picked up her lasso. "I'm getting much better, but Chad's just started to teach Taffy how to be a roping horse." She sighed. "She's not very good at it yet."

"But Taffy's quick," Clay said. "I've seen her. You

practice what Chad's been teaching her, and you'll have a chance."

Andi beamed at the cowboy. "I will!"

After that, the others peppered Diego with questions. The stars came out one by one until darkness settled over the yard. Still, no one left the porch.

A few minutes later Sid marched up the steps with a lantern. "You boys plan on working tomorrow?"

A hush fell over the group.

"Five o'clock comes mighty early these days," Sid went on. "The boys in number two have turned in. You better do the same."

"Yes, sir." The cowhands stood and stretched.

Sid looked at Andi. "You'd best be getting indoors too, missy. I reckon it's past your bedtime."

Andi didn't feel sleepy at all. *I don't have to get up early for anything.* School didn't even start until the Monday after the rodeo. *Besides, you're not Mother.*

She kept her words inside. For sure Mother would hear about it if Andi talked back to the Circle C foreman.

"Yes, sir." She grabbed her lasso and hopped off the porch.

Andi's heart thrummed with eagerness all the way back to the house. She banged through the kitchen door, past the dining room, and into the large sitting room. "Guess what!"

Mother looked up from where she and Melinda

sat paging through a ladies' fashion magazine. "Yes, dear?"

"Diego said there might be a calf-roping contest for the kids. Not the tie-down kind, but one that—"

"Oh, he did, did he?" Chad frowned.

Justin glanced up from the newspaper he was reading. "Really?"

Mitch grinned. "Sounds like fun."

"Hold on." Chad rose and held up his hands. "I haven't said anything about any contests for kids, and I'm the—"

"I know." Andi huffed. "You're the ranch boss. You get to decide everything, and it's not fair."

"Andrea," Mother warned. "That's enough. We only decided on the rodeo this evening. Settle down and give your brothers a chance to make plans."

"Yes, ma'am," Andi said quietly.

Yet inside she was far from settled. Her big plans might come crashing down at any moment.

It was hard enough being the youngest in the family without feeling left out most of the time. "Please, Chad," she begged. "Can't you have contests for somebody besides the ranch hands?"

Chad laughed. "This rodeo is *for* the ranch hands, Andi. Not for anybody else. Not for children, and especially not for little g—" He cleared his throat. "Never mind."

Mitch smiled. "Kids don't work cattle, Sis."

"I know they don't work cattle for real, but why not for fun? Like in a rodeo?" Andi put her hands on her hips. "I bet other ranchers and their cowhands have kids who would like to join in."

Chad shook his head. "I've got enough on my mind without having to . . ." His voice trailed off when he looked at Mother.

He sighed. "I'll think about it. I won't make any promises, but I'll talk to the other ranchers and see if—"

"Yippee!" Andi sailed across the room and threw her arms around Chad. "Mr. Flanders and Mr. Jenkins will agree. I know they will."

Without waiting for Chad's reply, Andi unwound her arms and said good night. She had plans to make. *Big* plans.

But first she needed a good night's sleep.

⊰ CHAPTER 5 ⊱

Rodeo Plans

Andi did not get a good night's sleep. Dozens of ropes twirled in her dreams. A lively calf tugged at the end of each imaginary lariat.

One calf grew bigger and bigger, large enough to yank Taffy away with him. Then Andi's filly changed into a bucking bronco. Taffy's golden body turned dark red. *Firebrand!*

Mother screamed.

Chad yelled, "Hang on!"

Andi was riding Firebrand, but only for a moment. She flew from the saddle and landed face-first in the dirt.

Andi woke with a gasp and sat up. Her head spun. Her hands shook. Lassos and calves and bucking broncos vanished.

Morning sunshine streamed in through the partly opened, glass-paned doors that led to the balcony. A soft breeze fluttered in Andi's face. Outside, the birds sang. The rooster crowed.

A horse whinnied, and she heard hoofbeats galloping past.

"It was only a dream," Andi told her heaving chest. "It's morning now."

She felt dizzy, so she waited for the dream to fade before getting out of bed. By the time she pulled on her shirt, overalls, and riding boots, the bad dream had shrunk to a small speck in the corner of her mind.

Andi was too excited to let any silly dream get in the way of her rodeo plans.

Me, ride Firebrand? She giggled all the way out of her room and down the stairs. She was still smiling when she sat down for breakfast.

Only Mother and Melinda remained at the table.

"What a sleepyhead you are today," Mother remarked. "Melinda called you for breakfast half an hour ago. When you didn't come, I told her to let you sleep."

Andi jabbed her fork into a stack of still-warm pancakes and slid two of them onto her plate. "I'm sorry, Mother. I was having a dream that seemed so real." She blurted out her story while she buttered the pancakes and dumped syrup on them.

Melinda laughed, but Mother didn't. "Listening

to the cowhands' tales just before bedtime is not a good idea."

"How else will I learn about the rodeo events?" Andi replied between bites of sweet, sticky pancakes. "Chad and Mitch sure won't tell me anything. They don't think kids should be part of any cowboy contests."

Mother rose with a smile. "Don't be so sure about that, Andrea. Give them a chance to talk to Mr. Flanders and Mr. Jenkins." She picked up her plate and coffee cup and headed for the kitchen. "When you finish eating, please get busy on your chores. It's well past sunup."

Andi swallowed before answering, "Yes, ma'am."

"I'm going upstairs to pack," Melinda said. Her voice tingled with excitement over her upcoming stay in the city.

Andi was left alone with half a pancake, a strip of bacon, and a glass of milk.

Luisa pushed through the dining room door a minute later. She greeted Andi cheerfully in Spanish and began to clear the table.

"Did you hear about the rodeo?" Andi asked Luisa in the same language.

"*Sí.*" She began to stack silverware and plates in the large dishpan she held in one arm. "Diego spoke of nothing else until late into the night."

Andi grinned up at the Mexican housekeeper. "It's going to be such fun!"

Luisa nodded. "I remember the old days when California belonged to Mexico. The *rancheros* hosted rodeos every season. But those days are gone." A slow smile crept over her face. "I am glad the *señores* are bringing it back. Perhaps it may become a yearly event."

"I hope so," Andi agreed. "But I'd like it even better if Chad and the other ranchers decided to let us kids join in."

"*Ay, no*, Miss Andrea!" Luisa set down her dishpan. "Rodeos are exciting to watch but very dangerous. You are just a little girl. Surely *Señor* Chad and your *mamá* will never permit such a thing."

Andi held back a hot reply. She had learned long ago not to talk back to Luisa. *She doesn't understand*, Andi thought. *Just like she doesn't understand how much I like to slide down the banister railing.*

"I don't want to compete *with* the cowboys," she said softly. "That would be silly. I'd lose." She pushed back her chair and stood up. "I only want some contests for the kids."

The wrinkled frown between Luisa's dark eyebrows told Andi that their housekeeper did not agree. Before Luisa could scold more, Andi thanked her for breakfast and hurried outside to the barn.

Andi's barn chores didn't take long. She made sure her filly had water and fresh hay. Then she took out the patches of soiled bedding and replaced them with clean straw.

Taffy trotted in from her paddock behind the barn and nickered a horsey good-morning.

Andi started right in. "A rodeo's coming up soon, girl. You're learning to be a roping horse. We just need a little more practice."

Taffy snorted her reply and dug into her alfalfa.

Andi grabbed a brush and began to groom her filly. "Chad and Mitch and the other ranchers just *have* to let us kids compete against each other."

Taffy chomped her hay and ignored Andi.

"Wait till the Bent Pine boys hear about this," Andi went on. "Richard's twelve. He'll for sure talk his father into it. Peter and Paul are ten. They'll want to compete too."

She smiled. Convincing the other ranchers didn't sound so hard. Not if their sons wanted to join in. Andi silently counted the number of children whose fathers worked for the three ranches.

"There's more than enough kids to have our own rodeo." Andi hugged Taffy. "It will be so much fun!"

She paused. For sure none of the grown-ups would let their children ride a bull or a wild bronco, but the older kids could rope a calf and maybe even tie one down. Others could team-rope a steer, and everybody could enter a horse race.

Wrapped up in rodeo plans, Andi took her time grooming Taffy. She found the comb and gently pulled the tangles from her filly's creamy-white mane. Taffy stood perfectly still while Andi combed out her tail.

Finally, Andi shook her head. "I can't stay out here any longer. Mother will have a fit if I don't straighten my room before lunchtime." She patted Taffy and left the barn.

Andi made a face. Dirty stalls were no fun to muck out. Messy rooms were worse. She went inside and plodded up the wide staircase. The door to Melinda's room hung open. Andi stopped and glanced inside.

Melinda's room was usually neat as a pin. Not today. Dresses and petticoats and hats and cloaks lay spread across her bed. A large trunk stood open. Melinda fluttered back and forth muttering to herself.

"What's wrong?" Andi asked, stepping inside.

Melinda plopped down on her bed. "I can't decide what to pack and what to leave behind."

Andi sat down beside her. "That's too bad." She was no help with that, so she changed the subject. "I've been thinking about the rodeo. Can I ask you a question?"

Melinda rolled her eyes and shrugged. "Sure."

"Do you think the Flanders girls would like to compete?"

"Liberty wouldn't be caught dead riding in something so unseemly as a roundup," Melinda said. "Neither would I."

She laughed. "You better get that silly-goose notion out of your head, Andi. Girls don't do such wild, reckless things. Even if Chad lets the other kids join in, Mother won't let *you* compete."

Andi bristled. "She—"

"She might let you wear overalls and help the boys brand calves now and then," Melinda went on. "But that's with our own people. When company comes Mother will make you wear a dress and watch the rodeo contests from a safe distance."

Andi sprang from the bed, fists clenched. "Mother *will* let me compete. You just wait and see!"

She stormed out of her sister's room without looking back.

❦ CHAPTER 6 ❧

Sadie's Great Idea

Andi stomped down the hallway. Tears stung her eyes. Just two weeks ago she and her big sister had enjoyed an afternoon together at the circus. A few days later they had ridden their horses and shared a picnic lunch.

Now all Melinda could talk about was acting like a lady and going away to school.

"You won't catch *me* at any ol' girls' school in San Francisco!" Andi hollered over her shoulder.

She ducked into her room, but her mind was not on cleaning it. Andi slammed her dresser drawers closed and made her bed. Then she sat down at her small desk and began to write down names on a piece of paper.

She didn't write Melinda's name—or any of the Triple L children. They were all girls.

Andi winced. Was Melinda right? Would Mother make Andi wear company clothes at a rodeo? Would only the boys on her list be allowed to ride and rope and race?

"No," she whispered. "Melinda doesn't know everything."

Gripping the pencil, Andi wrote her name. Miss Hall would have been proud of the perfectly formed letters.

Andi Carter Calf Roping

Andi added Sadie's name right below her own. The rest were boys who lived and worked on the three ranches. She also wrote down her friend Cory's name. Even though he lived in town, Cory would like to race. His horse, Flash, was fast as lightning.

When Mother called the family to lunch an hour later, Andi had twenty names on her list but only two were girls: Andi and Sadie. She folded the paper, jammed it into her overalls pocket, and went downstairs.

Andi kept quiet during lunch. No sense talking about a list if Chad said no.

Chad surprised her. "The Bent Pine and Triple L ranchers have agreed we should host a few special events for the younger boys." He rose to leave. "Happier now, little sister?"

Andi's heart skipped a beat at the word *boys*, but she nodded. "Thank you, Chad."

Chad grinned and ruffled Andi's hair. "You are most welcome. I reckon a rodeo should be fun for young and old alike. I'm glad you brought it up after all."

Whistling, he headed back to work.

Andi didn't feel like whistling. Her thoughts twirled faster than a lariat. Didn't Chad know she wanted to compete too? Why did he mention boys but not girls? Or had that idea come from Mr. Flanders or Mr. Jenkins?

Andi's stomach turned over. Most likely Chad knew Taffy was not a good enough roping horse to compete in the event.

I will change that, she decided quietly. *I'll start right after lunch.*

By the time the rodeo came around, Taffy would be an extra-good roping horse. Chad would have no reason not to let Andi take part in the kids' contests. Mother would surely agree if Chad agreed.

Even if Andi *was* a girl.

⊰ ⊱

Andi shaded her eyes and squinted against the bright afternoon sunlight. From a distance, her special spot looked the same as always. No cattle grazed there today, thank goodness. She slowed Taffy to a trot and pulled up next to her mucky fishing hole.

"'Bout time." Sadie lay slouched against the oak tree. She rose and stretched. "Where ya been?"

Andi made a face and dismounted. "Chores."

Sadie grunted. "Chores is just plumb foolishness. Lily helps Ma a bit, but the rest of us stay outta the way and do what we want."

A sliver of envy crept into Andi's thoughts. What fun it would be to never do any chores, not go to school, and just run and play all day long!

As quickly as her idea blossomed, common sense squashed it.

I don't really want to live like Sadie. Andi had seen their place—the dirt, the disorder, their ragged clothes and rickety buildings.

A few chores might do the Hollisters a world of good.

Sadie shook her. "What's the matter?"

Andi jerked back from her daydreaming and remembered why she'd come up here. "We're having a rodeo," she squealed.

Sadie wrinkled her forehead. "A what?"

"A roundup. Cowboy contests on our ranch."

Andi told her about the calf roping and horse racing, the bull riding and bronco busting, and all the other contests the cowboys would compete in. "And prizes and a barbecue and even ice cream."

Sadie's eyes opened wide. "I've never tasted ice cream."

"You will at the rodeo."

"Can anybody compete?" Sadie asked.

Andi nodded. "Even the kids. Chad told me so at lunch." She didn't add the part about the boys only. "I want to enter the calf-roping contest, but . . ." Her voice trailed off when she looked at Taffy.

"But what?"

"Taffy's not a very good roping horse yet," she whispered. Andi didn't want her filly to overhear her disloyal words. "I want to practice everything Chad's been teaching her. I can get her ready for the rodeo. I just need a little help."

"Zeke and Tom would get a real kick outta entering a rodeo." Sadie's eyes sparkled. "I betcha them two could stay on a buckin' bronco just as good as a grown-up cowhand. They're always tryin' to catch and ride wild mustangs with any ol' rope they find."

Andi hurried over to Taffy and fingered her lasso. "I have a good, stiff rope. I'll let your brothers practice with it if you'll help me get Taffy ready." She scrunched up her face. "It's no good lassoing fence posts, though. I need something that moves fast."

Sadie laughed. "Don't worry 'bout that. We got

plenty of runnin' critters." She scrambled up on Jep and motioned Andi to follow. "Come on!"

Andi swung into her saddle and nudged Taffy forward. She glanced sadly at the giant hoofprints that poked deep into the shallow stream and around her fishing hole. The mud was caked and dry.

Andi sighed. Maybe the winter rains would smooth things out again before next spring.

"Hurry up!"

Sadie's call urged Andi and Taffy to catch up. The girls loped toward the Hollister place. It was a long ride, but Sadie promised it would be worth it.

"Take a look," she said when they pulled their horses to a stop at the top of a small hill. "All the runnin' critters we need to practice lassoing."

Dozens of sheep grazed on the summer-dry grass in the valley below. Here and there, a few black sheep roamed. Half-grown lambs butted heads and leaped into the air.

Andi spotted Snowball, the bum lamb Sadie had tried to give her a few months ago. He looked small but healthy.

"Sh-sheep?" Andi stammered. "This is your great idea?"

Sadie nodded. "Look! There's Tom and Zeke over yonder. Wait till they hear the news." She put two fingers between her lips, whistled, and slammed her heels into Jep's sides.

The horse snorted and took off.

Andi followed at a slower pace. She looked at her lasso and frowned. If Chad ever found out that his little sister was practicing her roping skills on stinky sheep, he would laugh himself silly.

Sadie was right. Sheep were certainly running critters. But they were . . . *sheep*.

⊰ CHAPTER 7 ⊱

Sheep Trouble

When Andi finally caught up with her friend, it was clear that Sadie had told her brothers everything. The boys *yee-hawed* and galloped their horses in fast, tight circles. The sheep scattered.

Zeke and Tom yanked their horses to a stop beside Taffy.

"I hear you got yourself a fine lariat." Zeke eyed the coiled rope hanging around Andi's saddle horn. "Sadie says we can try it."

Andi nodded. "You need saddles to do it right, though."

"Naw," Tom said. "We wanna see how a fancy lariat works. Don't need no saddles for that."

Andi glanced at Jep. He wore a beat-up pony saddle over a raggedy blanket. When Sadie shifted

57

her weight, the saddle went with her. A strong calf might pull that saddle right off Jep if she dallied the rope around her saddle horn.

It was probably better if the Hollisters didn't use saddles after all.

Andi uncoiled her rope, made a big loop, and began to twirl the lasso over her head. Then she threw it. The rope circle fell neatly over Jep's head. Andi yanked, and the rope tightened.

Jep snorted and tossed his head, but he didn't fight the loop.

Zeke whistled and removed the rope from Jep's neck. "You sure make it look easy."

Zeke's words made Andi feel good all over.

"It *is* easy when your horse is standing still as a fence post." She coiled the rope back into her hands. "The hard part is lassoing a running calf. You gotta dally the rope around your saddle horn real quick so the horse can stop the calf. You don't want to get jerked off."

Andi cringed. She had been yanked out of her saddle more than once when she forgot to dally her rope. Or sometimes Taffy forgot to plant her feet. Then they all kept running until Andi let go of the rope.

Not good memories at all.

Sadie reached for Andi's lariat. "Lemme try."

Try she did, over and over. The loop went everywhere except around Taffy's head. Finally Sadie threw it to the ground, slid off Jep, and stomped on the rope. "Ain't no fair!"

Andi didn't laugh. She remembered how angry she'd felt yesterday when Sadie laughed at her for falling in the creek. She jumped down from Taffy's back, carefully looped her rope, and let Zeke have a turn.

Sadie's brothers were much better at roping. They dropped the lariat around Jep's neck. Then around Taffy's.

"Wish I had me one of these," Tom said when he pulled to a stop next to Andi. "Slick as grease to use. Better than ropes with slipknots."

"A slipknot?" Andi frowned. "A slipknot's no good. You need a honda knot. That way the rope can slide through without sticking."

"A what?" Zeke took a closer look at the small, looped knot. "Huh. That's some pretty fancy tying." He eyed Andi. "Can you make one for me?"

Andi shook her head. "I don't know how to tie a honda, but my brothers do. I could ask—"

"Nah." Zeke let out a disgusted breath and handed the rope back to Andi.

For the next hour the four of them took turns lassoing each other's horses. Sadie finally managed to throw a loop around Taffy. Then Andi nudged her filly into a trot and showed the others why they needed saddles.

Taffy behaved perfectly. When the rope dropped

over Jep's head, Andi dallied it around her saddle horn. Taffy stopped. The rope tightened.

Andi beamed. "Good girl!" Now, if only Taffy could remember her moves right up until the rodeo.

"I reckon it's time to practice on some actual *runnin'* critters now," Sadie said with a grin.

"I could gallop Trip," Zeke told Andi. "You could lasso him."

Andi shook her head. She better not try to rope a full-grown, running horse. It was too dangerous.

"Sheep are smaller," Sadie said. "More like a calf anyway."

Andi glanced at the quiet flock. "They don't look very interested in running."

Sadie laughed. "They will in a jiffy."

The Hollister children didn't need their horses to convince the sheep to move. They ran after them on foot, yelling and waving their arms. Their sheepdog joined in. He dashed back and forth, keeping the sheep together while the kids spooked them.

Andi lifted her lasso, nudged Taffy, and sprang into action.

It was like trying to herd cats.

Taffy turned this way and that, clearly not sure what she was being asked to do. Andi jounced from side to side. One foot came loose from her stirrup. She yelped and grabbed the saddle horn with both hands.

Once steady in the saddle, Andi focused on a

sheep that had been separated from the rest. Taffy headed for the running ball of wool. Andi threw her lariat before the sheep changed directions.

Bull's-eye!

The sheep jerked against the rope, fell onto its back, and lay still. Four legs stuck up from the woolly body. A moment later the sheep rolled this way and that, trying to right itself.

Andi sat on Taffy and stared at the silly creature. She had never seen anything like this before. No matter how hard it tried, the helpless sheep could not get up.

Sadie and her brothers finally joined her. They loosened the rope and helped the sheep to its feet.

It *baaed* all the way back to the flock.

The three Hollisters doubled over laughing. Tears rolled down their cheeks. They looked like they were having the time of their lives.

"Do it again, Andi!" Sadie howled between giggles.

Andi went along with it. For every sheep she managed to rope, four got away.

Taffy jerked to the right. She jerked to the left. She stopped and ran and turned until sweat darkened her neck. She stumbled over a small, grassy mound and snorted her unhappiness. *I'm not bred to go after these flighty sheep*, she seemed to be saying.

Andi agreed. Her legs hurt from gripping the saddle. Her arms ached from twirling her lasso and

then coiling it up when she missed. She felt as tired as Taffy looked.

The sheep were now bunched together in a close, tight group, *baaing* and running. The dog ran around in circles, barking. The sheep looked too frightened and exhausted to pay the herd dog any mind. A few sheep were limping.

Just then another sheepdog appeared from over a rise. A man on horseback followed. The horse paused at the top of the hill then broke into a gallop toward the sheep.

Andi's heart rose to her throat. *Mr. Hollister!*

Sadie, Zeke, and Tom turned toward the horse and rider. Their laughter died. They dashed toward their horses, but it was too late to run away.

Mr. Hollister whistled. The second sheepdog joined the first. Together they slowed the flock and circled them into a quivering, bleating mass. Mr. Hollister grunted then turned his wrath on the four children.

His first sentence included so many bad words that Andi shook with horror and fear.

"What in tarnation do ya think you're doin'?" he shouted next. "You're gonna run all the fat off them sheep with your shenanigans."

Nobody answered. The Hollister children stared at the ground.

Andi held her lasso in trembling hands. It was only partly coiled. The looped end lay on the ground.

For sure Mr. Hollister would figure out what they'd been up to.

She studied his angry face. He looked mad enough to whip them all.

His next words proved it. "I'm gonna tan your hides!"

"S-sorry, Pa," Tom stammered.

"You're gonna be a lot sorrier when you get home." He pointed toward the hills. "Now *git!*"

Sadie, Zeke, and Tom scrambled up on their horses.

Mr. Hollister's black gaze swept over the lasso then settled on Andi. "And you, girl. You got no call to treat my stock like they was cattle. Get back to your ranch. If I see you pesterin' these sheep again, I'll come lookin' for your brothers."

Andi blinked back terrified tears. No apology could get past her tight throat.

Mr. Hollister waved his arm. "Go on, I say. Get outta here."

Andi let her rope drop to the ground. She was too frightened to take the time to wind it up. She swung Taffy around and jabbed her in the sides.

Taffy leaped into a gallop, but it wasn't fast enough for Andi. She begged her filly to go faster . . . and faster, until she left the sheep and the kids and the furious Mr. Hollister far behind.

Only then did Andi allow herself a good cry.

⊰ CHAPTER 8 ⊱

Calf Trouble

Andi sat still as a mouse at the supper table. Thankfully, everyone was too busy talking about the rodeo to notice her silence.

When a loud knock rattled the front door, she nearly jumped a foot. A few months ago, Mr. Hollister had burst into their home. His fury had been directed at Chad that long-ago morning. She shivered. What about this time?

Andi squeezed her eyes shut. *Please don't let it be Mr. Hollister.*

To Andi's great relief, Luisa brought a folded paper and handed it to Chad. "A message from the Bent Pine, *señor.*"

Chad read the note and grinned. "Aha! Jenkins wants to include Firebrand in the bronc event after all."

"That ornery jug head?" Justin shook his head. "Bad idea."

"We've got a dozen good broncs already lined up," Mitch said. "Tell Jenkins no. We don't have a death wish. That horse can't be ridden."

Chad laughed. "Never a horse that can't be rode, little brother. Never a cowboy who can't be throwed—"

"This is supposed to be sporting fun," Mother broke in with a frown. "You and Ty Flanders and Phil Jenkins are starting to take this roundup much too seriously."

Chad dropped the note and picked up his spoon. "Why not? The men are excited. I say let Jenkins bring Firebrand."

Mother shook her head. "The Bent Pine can host their own rodeo if they want to include that horse. I won't have anybody killed on the Circle C on account of a silly competition."

Silence fell. It had only been two days, and now Mother's great idea of hosting a roundup seemed to be going wrong. Would she and Chad have an argument?

Andi swallowed. Chad might be the ranch boss, but Mother was . . . Well, Mother was right.

Chad glanced around the table. He passed over his sisters and looked at Mitch.

"I'm with Mother," Mitch said.

Justin raised an eyebrow and nodded.

Chad glared at his brothers then let out a deep breath and shrugged. "As you wish, Mother." He dug into his supper, but he didn't look happy.

Mother asked Melinda how her packing for the city was going, and rodeo talk died away.

Andi wanted to ask Mother and Chad about competing. Just as soon as her jitters faded from thinking Mr. Hollister was at the door, she had planned to bring up her question.

But not now. Rodeo talk was definitely over for the day—maybe even for the rest of the week.

Besides, Chad looked grumpy. Mother looked firm. It was not a good time to ask.

I will ask when it gets closer to rodeo day, she promised herself.

⚞ ⚟

Andi didn't see Sadie the next day. She wasn't surprised. Terrible things had probably happened to the Hollister children when they got home.

I might not ever see Sadie again, Andi thought two days later when she trotted toward her special spot. *Mr. Hollister is mean and scary.*

"Hey, Andi!" Sadie and Jep came barreling toward her.

Andi's mouth fell open. She pulled Taffy to a stop. "What are you doing here?"

"I got somethin' to show you. Took us all mornin', but wait till you see!" Her eyes twinkled as if nothing had gone wrong a few days before. "C'mon."

Andi didn't move. "B-but your pa. The sheep . . ." She paused, not sure how to bring up what had happened.

"Oh, *that*?" Sadie laughed. "Me and the boys lit out and hid the whole night." She shrugged. "When Pa figured out no sheep was dead, he cooled off and forgot about whippin' us. We came home mighty hungry, though."

Andi's head spun. What a strange family!

Sadie gave Andi no time for more questions. She kicked Jep and waved for Andi to follow. Thankfully, she didn't lead Andi anywhere near the Hollister sheep. She galloped Jep in the opposite direction.

"Where are we going?" Andi asked.

"Over yonder." The girls circled a clump of scraggly oaks and thick underbrush. A minute later they broke out into a wide, flat pasture that stretched for acres.

Andi didn't know if they were on Circle C range, Hollister land, or free range. Not far away, Tom and Zeke sat on saddled horses. A battered cowboy hat hung over Tom's forehead, and he twirled Andi's lariat. The boy looked like a real cowhand.

Especially since he was surrounded by four brown calves.

Andi sucked in her breath. The calves bawled and wandered here and there. They looked lonely for the rest of the herd. Where had they come from? Where were their mamas? How had the Hollisters managed to—

"Now you and me and the boys got real calves to practice on." Sadie smiled and pointed to Andi's saddle horn. "I see you got yourself another lariat. That's good."

Andi didn't answer. Her eyes were glued on the calves' brand marks:

"What's the matter?" Zeke pulled up beside Andi. "Your face is white."

Andi felt sick. "You rustled our calves!"

Zeke laughed. "This ain't no cattle rustlin'. *You're* here, ain't ya? You're a Carter, and those are your calves." He shrugged as if it all made perfect sense.

Maybe it did, but Andi didn't think Chad would see it that way. Neither would Mitch. Or Justin or Mother, probably. *This is a terrible idea!*

Tom held up the lariat Andi had left behind in her hurry to get away from Mr. Hollister. "Ropin' calves is easy as pie with this-here lasso. I s'pose you want it back."

Andi nodded. She took it and handed Tom the lariat she'd brought from home. "Here's an old one nobody uses anymore. You can use it, but not on these calves. Chad will have our hides."

The Hollister boys just laughed and went back to their sport. They missed a lot, and their horses acted confused, but Tom and Zeke kept at it. They took turns with the lariat.

Andi watched, helpless. "Take those calves back where they belong," she ordered.

The boys ignored her.

"You asked for help gettin' ready for the calf rop-ing." Sadie pointed to the calves. "They're here now. You better practice if you want your filly to have half a chance at winnin'."

Andi watched Zeke twirl his rope. Maybe he was right about the calves. In a way they were just as much Andi's as they were anybody else's on the Circle C. Why not practice on them?

"Come on, Taffy." She gripped her lariat and dug her heels into Taffy's sides. "Let's show the Hollister boys how it's done."

Andi's golden filly started out strong, but she soon turned skittish. Half the time she forgot to plant her feet. Instead, she followed the roped calf around until the poor animal was too tired to run any longer.

Andi gritted her teeth. Taffy should know what

to do without Andi telling her. Patches always knew what to do. "These calves wouldn't sneak by me if I was riding Patches," she muttered, hoping Taffy couldn't hear her.

Just then, Taffy stopped short. Andi yelped and grabbed the saddle horn to keep her seat. "Why did you do that? We weren't close enough to rope him."

Taffy flattened her ears, and the calf kept running.

A few minutes later, Andi nearly lost a thumb. Her fingers slipped while she dallied the rope, and her thumb got caught. Luckily, Taffy didn't stop, and the rope stayed loose.

At the end of two hours, Andi was exhausted. Her hands burned even through her gloves. She had never worked so hard in her life.

Andi hardly ever missed a toss when she rode Patches. On Taffy, she missed half the time. Calf roping was definitely a team event—horse and rider.

Mostly the horse, Andi admitted. *And Taffy's mighty green.*

She still had time to practice, but would it do any good? The calves were now so tired that they stood still and let anybody rope them. One calf lay dozing in the sun.

Dumb calves.

CHAPTER 9

Taffy Trouble

Every afternoon that week and most of the next Andi rode Taffy out to the pasture. Zeke and Tom always managed to round up fresh Circle C calves to lasso. The boys hollered and hooted and roped calves left and right.

It wasn't hard to figure out that Zeke's horse, Trip, had once been a roping horse. Or maybe the gray pony was a fast learner. For sure Zeke was. With Andi's old lariat circling his head, Zeke caught the calf of his choice nine times out of ten.

The Hollister boy had a good chance of winning the kids' calf-roping contest.

Andi's chances were not as good, even though Taffy was improving with practice. The filly was quick on her feet, but she wore out faster than Trip and the other horses.

"It's all right." Andi rubbed Taffy's neck and spoke softly. "You only have to chase the calf one time in the arena. Not over and over like we've been doing every day."

Taffy didn't nicker her agreement. She didn't nod or shake her mane. Instead, the palomino's head drooped in the hot afternoon sun. Her sides heaved. One foot pawed the ground.

Worry tickled Andi's stomach. She knew what Chad would say if he saw Taffy right now.

You're overworking your horse.

Chad never spent hours working Taffy like Andi had done all week. He worked the young horse in short spurts. Then Andi and Taffy rode for fun.

Andi slid from the saddle and threw her arms around Taffy's neck. A big lump clogged her throat. "I'm sorry, Taffy," she whispered.

Sadie yanked Jep to a stop beside Andi. "What's wrong?"

"I think I better go home. Taffy needs to rest after all this roping practice. I don't want to wear her out before the rodeo." Andi's heart squeezed. "Besides, I can't let Chad see her like this."

Sadie nodded. "You're right. She don't look so good."

Andi climbed into the saddle, wound up her lasso,

and dropped it over the saddle horn. "Zeke and Tom better put those calves back. If they sneak any more it'll be *real* cattle rustling and"—she swallowed—"I'll tell Chad."

Sadie's eyes grew round. "Reckon I'll see ya at the rodeo then."

"Yeah, this Saturday. It'll be fun." Andi sighed and turned Taffy toward home.

All of a sudden the rodeo didn't sound like any fun at all. Not if Taffy was too worn out to compete.

Andi's stomach tickled again. Taffy showed no interest in galloping or loping. She dragged her feet. Once in a while she stumbled.

Twice Andi stopped to look at Taffy's feet. No pebbles were stuck in her hooves. Everything looked fine, but Andi kept her filly at a slow gait until they got home.

Even before they trotted into the yard, Andi could see how busy the cowhands had been the past few days.

Not far from the shady back yard a huge corral was going up. Hammers rang as nails were pounded into the spilt-wood railings that stretched between fence posts.

It was the biggest arena Andi had ever seen—as big as ten corrals. She pulled Taffy to a standstill and watched wide-eyed when another wagonload of slim tree trunks lumbered to a stop.

"They had to go a long way up in the hills to cut those trees," she told Taffy.

Taffy snorted, and her ears pricked up. She turned her head toward the giant enclosure.

"That's where everybody will compete." Andi pointed to a newly built gate. "See there? A calf will be let in, and then *whoosh!* You gotta run fast as you can to catch up so I can rope it." She patted Taffy. "Think you'll be rested by then?"

Taffy's head bobbed up and down.

Andi's spirits rose, and she shaded her eyes. Roundup must be over. Most of the cowhands were working here instead of out on the range. Behind the new arena, dozens of flags waved in the breeze. They were tied to valley oaks to mark the racetrack.

Andi grinned in delight. Racing took no special skills. Once Taffy had rested, they could easily compete in the horse race.

The sound of whinnying, snorting, and bellowing caught Andi's ear. "Come on, girl. Let's go see what that's all about."

She prodded Taffy past the new arena and toward a number of corrals and round pens. They held calves, steers of all sizes, and wild-eyed horses in every color. Scary-looking bulls glared at her from inside their small, separate pens.

"Get away from there, Miss Andi!" Sid's voice crackled. "Ain't no place for you to play."

"I'm not playing," Andi said. "I'm looking."

"Uh-uh." Sid grabbed Taffy's bridle and tugged her away from the rodeo pens. "You never know when one of them ornery critters might bust through the fence."

He let go and slapped Taffy on the rump. "Now, get out of here."

Taffy obeyed, and Andi went along for the ride. Her filly slowed down in front of the barn.

Andi dismounted. She pulled the reins over Taffy's head and led her inside. "You're happy to see your stall, aren't you, girl?"

Taffy nickered.

As usual, Andi had to find somebody to help her with Taffy's saddle. She wasn't strong enough to lift the heavy piece of tack herself. She loosened the cinch and glanced around for a ranch hand.

Not far away, the door to the tack room opened then banged shut. Andi heard footsteps.

"Need some help?"

Andi whirled. *Uh-oh.*

Chad stood a few feet away. Without waiting for an answer, he lifted Andi's saddle and dropped it over a nearby railing. The saddle blanket slipped off. Chad caught it and flung it down next to the saddle.

He grinned. "There you go. Did you have a nice ri—" He caught his breath, and his smile faded.

Andi gulped. Taffy's bare back and sides were dark with sweat.

Chad ran his hand along Taffy's damp neck and sides. He looked into her eyes.

Taffy shuddered. She dropped her head and let out a long, tired whicker.

"Easy, girl." Chad rubbed her nose. "Andi, *what have you been doing?*"

She felt a hot flush spread up her neck. "Riding."

Chad shook his head. "What *else* have you been doing?"

"Roping," Andi quickly replied. "You never said I couldn't."

Silence fell. Chad chewed his lip, glanced at Taffy, then looked at Andi. "How *much* roping?"

Andi didn't answer. She didn't have to. Taffy's slumped body and tired eyes told Chad the whole story.

"For the contest on Saturday?" he asked.

Andi nodded. "I want to compete in the calf roping for kids. I'm good with a lasso."

This was not the way she'd planned to ask, but it was too late now.

"Yes," Chad said slowly. "You're good. Taffy, though, is too young and too green."

He folded his arms across his chest. "Why didn't you ask to borrow Pal or Patches? They're older, more experienced roping horses."

Andi looked down at her boots. "I wanted to surprise everybody."

"Instead, it looks like you've worked your horse into a sorry state."

Fear clutched Andi's belly. Her head snapped up. "Will she be all right?"

"Yes, with plenty of rest and good care," Chad said. "But she's in no shape for any rodeo contests—not even a short race. If you hadn't kept this a secret from me, I would have let you enter on Patches. But not now."

Tears pricked Andi's eyes. No race. No calf roping.

A sob caught in her throat, but she swallowed it. No rodeo.

⊰ CHAPTER 10 ⊱

Rodeo Day

Rodeo day dawned clear, bright, and not too hot. It was a perfect day for everybody—everybody but Andi. The quiet talk she and Mother had last night didn't help Andi feel better about not joining in today's contests.

But she had promised Mother she would try to make the best of it.

Wagons and buggies began arriving shortly after sunup. Women wearing bonnets and straw hats spilled from the vehicles. Their arms were heaped with blankets and baskets of food.

"Howdy, Andi!" Richard Jenkins jumped down from the Bent Pine wagon and untied his spotted horse.

Andi waved, but she couldn't bring herself to

smile. A neatly coiled lasso hung around Richard's saddle. It looked like he would be entering the kids' calf-roping contest.

Andi sighed. She stood on the back porch with freshly combed braids, hair ribbons, and wearing her red-plaid dress. Her wide-brimmed hat hung down her back. The string dug into her neck, but she didn't care.

Company clothes. She made a face.

Cowboys dressed in their best shirts and leather chaps pranced by on their horses. They *yee-hawed* and bragged to each other while they headed for the animal pens.

A tiny smile parted Andi's lips. The horses were slicked up fancier than their riders. Some mounts showed off braided manes and tails. Others wore freshly polished saddles.

Andi skipped out of the way when she heard Luisa calling. The Circle C housekeeper had found a dozen relatives to help with the task of setting up the food tables and serving the barbecue. Now Luisa flew through the back door. She narrowly missed Andi and scolded her in sharp Spanish.

Andi jumped off the porch and followed the busy housekeeper. Mother and the other women were covering long boards with clean white sheets and tablecloths. A tall barrel with a round lid stood near the end of one table. Sid dumped ice chips into it.

Andi peeked inside. Lemon slices floated on top of gallons of lemonade.

Sid grinned. "Better taste it, Miss Andi. Make sure it's not too sweet or too sour." He held up the dipper.

Andi perked up. She sipped the cool drink and smiled. "It's just right."

Sid ruffled her hair and left whistling.

A few minutes later, Cory and his family pulled in. Flash was tied to the back of their buggy. Cory's chestnut horse had been groomed until his reddish coat shone.

"Thanks for telling me about the rodeo last Sunday," Cory said when Andi greeted him. "I've been racing every spare minute." He wrinkled his forehead. "Why are you all slicked up? You can't race in that getup."

"I'm not racing," Andi said. "Taffy doesn't feel well."

Cory's eyes opened wide. "Yippee! Now I've got a chance to win." Then he stammered, "Uh . . . I-I didn't mean it, Andi. I'm sorry you and Taffy can't race."

Andi shrugged. "I'll cheer for you and Flash," she promised.

By the time ten o'clock rolled around, the ranch was swarming with guests. News about the Circle C rodeo had spread like wildfire up and down the valley.

Some visitors came from as far away as Visalia, forty miles to the south.

Wagons, buggies, carriages, and horses choked the yard. Children of all ages dashed back and forth. Two little Mexican girls wearing their brothers' britches led their ponies toward the racing area.

Everybody is competing today, Andi thought sadly. *Everybody but me.*

She glanced toward the makeshift seating near the large arena. Not everybody was competing. Clumps of girls and young ladies wearing bright colors giggled and eyed the handsome cowboys.

Andi rolled her eyes and joined them.

Sid and two others hurried toward the arena. Each carried a stopwatch. They sat atop the corral railing as the rodeo judges.

In spite of Andi's heavy heart, she clapped with the rest of the crowd when Chad announced bronc riding as the first event. Fifteen cowboys lined up near the gate. One by one, each man burst into the arena riding a crazy-wild horse.

There was only one rule in bronc riding. Whoever stayed on the longest won.

Andi forgot her own troubles when Mitch tore into the arena. Her heart leaped with excitement. The bronc crow-hopped, twisted, and zigzagged until Andi got dizzy from watching.

"Stay on, Mitch!" she yelled.

Beside her, Melinda hollered louder than Andi.

Just then, Mitch's stirrup snapped. He flew backward and crashed to the ground. The horse kicked out its hind feet, narrowly missing Mitch.

The crowd gasped. Melinda screamed.

Andi went white. She ran to the arena and clutched the railing. "Mitch, Mitch!"

Mother gently pulled Andi away. "Hush, Andrea. He's all right. Look. They're corralling the horse and keeping him away from your brother."

Sure enough, two riders expertly drove the wild horse from the arena. Another cowhand helped Mitch to his feet. He shook his head, found his hat, and waved to Mother and Andi. Then he limped out of the arena.

Andi's heart slowed down. She followed Mother back to their seats.

The next man mounted a minute later. Another cowhand whipped off the blindfold and let the bronc loose. The Circle C hand, Clay, stayed in the saddle like a sticky burr.

He didn't stay on long enough, though. A Bent Pine cowboy won the contest by two seconds. Andi groaned her disappointment.

The cowboy contests flew by like whirlwinds. Bull riding followed bronc riding. The Triple L ranch won that event. Andi covered her eyes when one of the bulls nearly trampled a thrown rider.

Andi hollered until her throat felt raw during the team-roping contest. She yelled louder when Chad and Mitch went after a steer together. Chad threw his lariat first. It landed around the steer's horns. Quick as a flash, he dallied his rope and turned the large animal so Mitch could rope its hind feet.

Then it was over. The steer lay stretched helplessly on the ground between the two horses.

"Time!" Sid yelled. "Six seconds."

Andi gasped. That was fast. She clapped and yelled, "We won, we won!"

In all the excitement, Andi forgot how unhappy she'd been this morning—until Chad called a break from the cowboy events.

"Calf roping for the kids," he announced.

Andi's enjoyment died. She watched a line of horses gather near the gate and wished with all her heart that she and Taffy waited there too. "May I watch up close?" she asked.

Mother nodded, and Andi hurried to stand by the railing.

She watched through blurred tears while boy after boy galloped through the gate. Each one tried to throw his rope around a lively calf.

Three boys missed. The others caught the calf during their turns, but their horses looked as slow as three-legged mules. Ten-year-old Paul Jenkins chased his calf twice around the ring before lassoing it.

"They might as well chase those calves on foot," Andi muttered. She slumped against the railing. "Tom and Zeke are much faster."

But Sadie's brothers were not here to prove it.

Richard Jenkins won the event. He had a fast time, but Andi knew she and Taffy could have done it faster.

"Tie-down roping for the cowhands," Chad announced.

Andi perked up. Would the Circle C cowhands rope and tie up a calf's legs quicker than anybody else? Wyatt was mighty good at it. She'd watched him rope, tie, and brand calves many times.

The first contestant mounted his horse. The crowd hushed.

Then a loud voice broke into the silence. "What in the world is *that*?"

ᵈ CHAPTER 11 ᵇ

Unwelcome
Guests

The question came from Mr. Jenkins. He stood at the east end of the large arena, shaded his eyes, and gazed toward the foothills.

Andi climbed to the top railing to see what the Bent Pine rancher was looking at.

A small group of horses, a wagon, and people were headed toward the ranch. Dust puffed up around them. It made it hard to see who they were.

Nobody had to see these visitors, though. A familiar and unwelcome sound filled the air. *Baa, baa!*

Sheep!

All activity inside and outside the arena halted. The cowboys waiting to compete sat stock-still in their saddles. The two hundred guests turned to gawk at the approaching hill people.

"They got some nerve," a cowhand standing near Andi muttered.

Mr. Jenkins stomped alongside the arena railing until he found Chad. "Whose idea was it to invite those no-accounts?" He kept his voice low, but Andi heard him.

She cringed.

"Don't look at me," Chad shot back, red-faced. "I didn't invite them."

The Hollister clan stopped a short distance from the arena. "Howdy!" Mr. Hollister called. "Heard you-all was havin' a ro-dee-o."

The bleating from a dozen sheep grew louder. A sheepdog kept them in place.

"We brung a few sheep for the littlest young'uns to ride." Mr. Hollister chuckled. "It's plumb fun to watch 'em bounce around all over the place."

The rodeo crowd murmured their disapproval. Sheep? At a rodeo?

Mr. Flanders from the Triple L hurried over to Chad. "This is a cattlemen's event, not a sheepherder's dirty gathering."

"I can smell those walking vermin clear across the yard," Mr. Jenkins added. "What's going on?" He plugged his nose. "Send them away."

Mitch, Sid, and the foremen from the two other

ranches joined their bosses. "They gotta clear out, Chad," Sid warned. "You know how quick this could get out of hand."

From her perch a few yards away, Andi's stomach turned over. *What have I done?*

Chad had not invited the Hollisters, but the other ranchers were blaming him. They looked shocked and angry.

When Justin joined the ranchers' huddle, Andi knew things were boiling. But even her smart, calm big brother might not be able to keep the Circle C rodeo from exploding into a range war.

The whole rodeo is ruined, and it's my fault.

She glanced at the Hollisters. Their eager greetings had died away. They stood bunched together as if they feared the worst. Even mean-looking Mr. Hollister seemed unsure of what to do or say. His family was outnumbered by the cattlemen and valley folks.

Andi saw Sadie's frightened look. She pasted a smile on her face and waved to her friend.

Sadie did not wave back.

"Hold on," Chad said just then. He left the ranchers and came over to where Andi sat on the arena fence. He glanced at the Hollisters. Then he looked at Andi. He didn't say anything.

Andi caught her breath. *He knows I invited them.*

"I'm sorry, Chad," she whispered.

Waves of sadness washed over Andi. Everything had gone so well until Sadie and her family showed up. Andi had enjoyed watching the rodeo almost as much as if she had competed in it.

But now?

"I guess I shouldn't have—" The words choked in her throat. Tears spilled.

Chad smiled at her. "Hey, there. It's not your worry."

"Who ever heard of sheepherders at a cattlemen's roundup?" someone yelled from a group of cowboys.

Chad stiffened. He put his arm around Andi and hugged her. Then he whirled on the outspoken cowhand.

"Whoever heard of *anything* we're doing here today? There aren't any rules about who can be here and who can't. Or even what contests we plan." He looked at Mother sitting in the stands. "I was reminded the other night that this rodeo is supposed to be *fun*."

"Smelling sheep ain't no fun," a cowboy shouted.

Other cowhands added their thoughts. None were kind. Most demanded that the dirty sheepherders leave at once. "Before we run 'em off!"

Andi buried her head against Chad's shoulder and sobbed.

No matter how it ended, this special day was

spoiled. The picnic tables were loaded down with food. The aroma of roasting beef drifted past her.

No barbecue now. Everybody would go home angry, hungry, and upset.

Worst of all, the pounds and pounds of ice Clay and Wyatt and Sid had chipped away to make ice cream was all for nothing. Sadie had never tasted ice cream. Andi had promised she would today.

Not anymore.

Chad's arm tightened around Andi. "Don't cry," he whispered in her ear. "I'll fix this. The Hollisters can stay."

"But how? Everybody is so—"

"You leave that to me." Chad yanked a bandana from his pocket. "Here. Wipe your face."

Andi obeyed. She sniffed back her tears and sat still. Inside, though, she was shaking.

Would Chad tell every rancher and cowhand and guest that his baby sister had made a mess of things? That the Hollisters had come because she'd invited them?

Don't let a silly child ruin our rodeo.

The words sounded horrible in Andi's mind. But what else could Chad say to keep the cattlemen from chasing the Hollisters off the ranch?

By now most of the cowboys had gathered inside the arena. They muttered and shot dark looks at the Hollisters.

In return, a shotgun appeared in Mr. Hollister's hand. His black brows came together in a deep scowl. "Fine way to greet a neighbor," he growled.

Chad pulled Mr. Flanders and Mr. Jenkins aside. They spoke together in low voices.

A few minutes later Chad called to the men in the arena. "All right. That's enough. You've had your say. Now get ready for the next event."

The cowboys' mouths dropped open. They stared at the three ranchers standing side by side.

"You heard him," Mr. Flanders said when the men didn't move.

"Yes, sir." They broke up and found their horses.

Chad turned to the bystanders. "The Bent Pine, Triple L, and Circle C ranches are welcoming our unexpected guests. Anyone who has forgotten the Golden Rule is free to leave."

The restless crowd grew quiet. It appeared that the words of Jesus—treat others as you would want others to treat you—had found their way into many hearts.

Chad sniffed and smacked his lips. "I hope you all stay. Sure would hate for anybody to miss out on the barbecue."

Chuckles rippled through the gathering.

The shotgun in Mr. Hollister's hand disappeared into the back of his wagon.

"Well, boss, when you put it that way," a cowhand yelled, "I ain't leavin' before I get a bite of that beef."

More laughter.

"I reckon the Golden Rule won't hurt none of us today," Mr. Flanders said. He winked at Andi.

Andi ducked her head. Chad had told the other ranchers, after all. But nobody else needed to know. She sighed in relief.

Then she hopped off the railing and ran over to welcome Sadie and her family to the rodeo.

☙ CHAPTER 12 ☙

Hurrah for the Rodeo!

Chad sent two cowhands to clear out a pen for the sheep. "That'll keep them out of sight until the rest of the contests are over." He shrugged. "Maybe everybody will forget about them and the Hollisters' sheep-riding offer. Best I can do for now."

Chad's words smoothed the cattlemen's ruffled feathers. They grinned and relaxed. Sheepherders didn't seem so bad so long as nobody had to put up with their sheep.

Some kindhearted townsfolk made room in the stands for the Hollister family. They crowded in, scuffling and scrambling for good spots.

Andi knew a hundred eyes were watching her when she squeezed in beside Sadie. She didn't care.

Chad had stood up for her today. He had convinced the other ranchers to include the unwelcome guests.

I'm not sorry Sadie's my friend, Andi thought, scooting closer.

It was a tight fit. Eight scruffy children, their parents, and Granny took up an entire bench seat. They hooted and hollered and stomped their feet during the tie-down calf roping.

Zeke and Tom didn't seem to care a bit that they had missed the kids' roping. They dashed to their horses when the racing events started.

Andi cheered for Cory until Sadie jabbed an elbow in her side. "Why're you cheerin' for that town kid?"

Andi didn't answer. It didn't matter. Neither Cory nor the Hollister boys won. Eleven-year-old Paco Ortega, whose father worked for the Bent Pine, came in first by a nose.

When the official rodeo events ended an hour later, Chad stood in the middle of the arena. "We have a last-minute addition to our roundup," he announced. "A trick-riding display." He waved an arm then hiked himself over the railing to stay out of the way.

Six horses burst through the wide-open gate and galloped around and around the arena.

Andi's mouth dropped open. So *this* is where Sadie had disappeared a few minutes before.

From thirteen-year-old Lily to five-year-old Jonah,

six of the Hollister children showed off their skills. They stood on their horses. They hung from their saddles. They ran and mounted galloping horses.

Zeke even crawled around his horse's belly at a breakneck gait.

The crowd gasped.

"They're all touched in the head," one onlooker muttered. "Crazy hill folk trying to get their young'uns killed."

Not one Hollister child slipped or was thrown. When their act ended, they lined up, held hands, and bowed.

Everyone broke into wild clapping and cheering.

The Hollisters mounted their horses and sped away through the gate.

Andi was left breathless at the display. Sadie and her brothers and sister were better than any of the circus acts she'd seen last month. And Sadie had never said a word about it!

What an exciting way to end the rodeo!

But the rodeo was not over.

Chad hopped into the arena, loosened his lariat, and began twirling it. Mr. Flanders and Mitch joined him. Together they spun the rope around themselves and jumped in and out of it in perfect rhythm with each other.

The crowd clapped in time to the fancy roping and roared their approval when it ended.

Andi beamed with pride at her clever brothers. Surely this was the last act. It couldn't get any better.

Mitch and Mr. Flanders moved away, but Chad stood in the center of the arena and looked into the stands. When he saw Andi, he waved at her. "Come here."

Andi felt red creep up her neck and into her cheeks. What was Chad up to? She looked at Mother. "What does he want?"

Mother's slight frown told Andi that she didn't know what Chad was up to either. "Go ahead," she said.

Chad waved Andi over, more firmly this time.

She jumped down from her seat, squeezed between the railings, and hurried over to Chad. When she turned around, her heart skipped a beat. From here, the two hundred bystanders looked more like two thousand.

"Can I go back and sit down?" she asked.

"Not a chance." Chad bent down to Andi's level. "You've had a double disappointment today," he said. "I'm sorry. For one thing, you couldn't compete."

Andi squirmed. Why bring that up now?

"I also saw how much it hurt you when everybody treated the Hollisters badly," Chad said. "You think you ruined the rodeo by inviting them, but you didn't. Their stunt riding was a real treat and worth having them here."

Chad clasped Andi's hand and drew her with him toward the far end of the arena. Sky waited, tied to a fence post. "I've changed my mind about you not roping today. You have a gift with the lariat."

Andi wrinkled her forehead. He changed his mind? *Too late, big brother. The calf-roping event is over.*

"Would you like to give a roping display on Sky?" Chad asked. "Like the Hollisters did with their fancy riding? It's not the same as riding Taffy, but Sky won't let you down."

Andi gaped at Chad. She couldn't speak. She couldn't breathe. She glanced behind her shoulder. Mitch and Mr. Flanders were entertaining the crowd with more fancy roping.

"It will be the last act of the rodeo," Chad went on. "The finale. Afterward, we'll enjoy the barbecue. What do you say? Can you do it?" He grinned. "Even in a dress? There's no time to change your clothes."

Tingles raced up and down Andi's arms. *Can I do this?* Her voice came back in a flash. "Oh, yes, Chad. I can do it."

"I thought so." Chad tossed Andi up on Sky.

Andi ignored the billowing ruffles of her skirts flying and the fact that somebody might see her bloomers. Then a sliver of uncertainty made her pause. What would Mother say about her daughter riding astride in a dress?

Andi glanced into the stands. Mother wasn't frowning, so it must be all right.

Chad handed Andi his lariat and adjusted the stirrups for her short legs. "I want you to show all these folks what a Carter can do with a rope." He winked. "You hear me?"

Andi sat high up on Sky, fingering the rope. Her throat felt dry as the dirt in the arena. Her heart was thumping out of control.

She loosened the lariat until she had a big loop. Then Andi gripped Sky's reins with her free hand and nodded. "I will, Chad."

Chad patted her leg then hurried back to the middle of the arena. Mitch and Mr. Flanders stepped aside.

The crowd clapped, but Chad raised his hands to quiet them.

"She may be young and the only girl to toss a rope today," he said when they settled down, "but nine-year-old Andrea Carter will show you how we do things on the Circle C ranch."

He motioned to one of the men standing at the gate. It swung open, and a lively calf burst headlong into the arena.

Sky didn't need Andi to tell him what to do. The buckskin horse launched himself after the calf like a cannonball.

Andi didn't need Chad to tell *her* what to do

either. She twirled the rope around her head three times and let it go.

The loop landed neatly over the calf's head and settled around his neck. Andi dallied the rope, Sky planted his feet, and the calf stopped short in its tracks.

The crowd leaped to their feet. They yelled and clapped.

Andi looked past the clapping people and into her mother's smiling face. Even Melinda was jumping up and down. Her straw hat had fallen off in her excitement.

Andi grinned. *Not very ladylike.*

"Good for you!" Melinda cupped her hands and shouted over the applause.

Andi unwound her rope and let it drop. She beamed her happiness. Nothing else her brother could have said or done today would have told Andi how much Chad loved her.

Even when she messed up.

Chad ran up to the horse and rider. He was beaming too. "That was a great time, little sister. Six seconds."

Andi's heart swelled with love for her family. She wished Sky knew how to take a bow. Instead, she stood up in Sky's saddle, took her own bow, then jumped into Chad's waiting arms.

What a perfect ending to the Circle C rodeo!

History Fun
Rodeos

Rodeos played an important part of ranching life in the Old West. California passed a law in 1851 that required every rancher to hold at least one rodeo a year. Did the state want ranchers to create fun cowboy competitions?

Not at all. The rodeo was not a sporting event in the 1800s like it is today. The rodeo law was meant to encourage ranchers to meet for the purpose of separating their cattle and horses. During these roundups, the livestock were examined, divided up, and branded.

In addition to dealing with so many mixed-up cattle, the Spanish *vaqueros* showed off their amazing horsemanship. They chose the wildest broncos to break. They rode bulls and roped calves. Wealthy ranchers and all their attendants showed up and stayed for the unlimited hospitality offered.

Ranch versus ranch cowboy contests gradually sprang up. Bronc riding, bull riding, and roping contests later began to appear at racetracks and fairs.

Buffalo Bill Cody created the first rodeo for sport in 1882, along with his famous Wild West show. Others followed Cody's example, and the professional rodeo was born. However, the word *rodeo* was hardly ever used for this American cowboy sport.

Early rodeos were a mishmash of events that could last all day. Not only might they include bronc riding and calf roping, but also Pony Express races, nightshirt races, and even a football game! Trick riding and fancy roping were also popular. The cowboys did not know the events offered or the rules until they paid their entry fees.

Today's professional rodeo is organized, and everybody follows the same rules. It includes five events: calf roping, bareback and saddle bronc riding, bull riding, and steer wrestling. They also have the option to include steer roping and team roping.

This cowboy sport today goes by different names: rodeo, roundup, stampede, or frontier days. Whatever its name, a rodeo is a great way to go back in time and glimpse the life of an Old West cowboy.

**For more Andi fun,
download free activity pages
at CircleCSteppingStones.com.**

Susan K. Marlow is always on the lookout for a new story, whether she's writing books, teaching writing workshops, or sharing what she's learned as a homeschooling mom. Susan is the author of several series set in the Old West—ranging from new reader to young adult—and she enjoys relaxing on her fourteen-acre homestead in the great state of Washington. Connect with the author at CircleCSteppingStones.com or by emailing Susan at SusanKMarlow@kregel.com.

Leslie Gammelgaard, illustrator of the Circle C Beginnings and Circle C Stepping Stones series, lives in beautiful Washington state where every season delights the senses. Along with illustrating books, Leslie inspires little people (especially her four grandchildren) to explore and express their creative nature through art and writing.